Mr. Fletcher
Room #

Mrs. Lewis
Room G

SALMON MOON

SALMON MOON

BY MARK KARLINS

ILLUSTRATED BY HANS POPPEL

SIMON & SCHUSTER BOOKS FOR YOUNG READERS
Published by Simon & Schuster
New York London Toronto Sydney Tokyo Singapore

SIMON & SCHUSTER BOOKS FOR YOUNG READERS
Simon & Schuster Building, Rockefeller Center
1230 Avenue of the Americas, New York, New York 10020
Text copyright © 1993 by Mark Karlins. Illustrations copyright
© 1993 by Hans Poppel. All rights reserved including the right of
reproduction in whole or in part in any form. SIMON & SCHUSTER
BOOKS FOR YOUNG READERS is a trademark of Simon & Schuster.
Designed by Lucille Chomowicz.
The text for this book is set in 14 point Palatino.
The illustrations were done in watercolor.
Manufactured in the United States of America
10 9 8 7 6 5 4 3 2 1
Library of Congress Cataloging-in-Publication Data
Karlins, Mark.   Salmon moon / by Mark Karlins : illustrated by
Hans Poppel.   p.   cm.   Summary: Mr. Lutz, Mrs.
Mankowitz, and her granddaughter liberate a wonderful live
salmon from a Coney Island fish market and return it to the sea.
[1. Salmon—Fiction.   2. Jews—Fiction.   3. Coney Island
(New York, N.Y.)—Fiction.]   I. Poppel, Hans, ill.   II. Title.
PZ7.K14245Sal   1993   [E]—dc20   92-15702   CIP
ISBN: 0-671-73624-8

For my mother and father with love—M.K.

_____

For Ken—H.P.

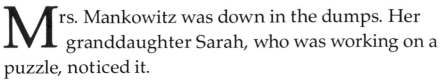

Mrs. Mankowitz was down in the dumps. Her granddaughter Sarah, who was working on a puzzle, noticed it.

Mr. Lutz, when he stopped by for a glass of tea, noticed it too. "So?" Mr. Lutz began, "what's with you?"

"Oy, if only I knew," she said. "Besides, who wants to listen to troubles?"

"I'll listen," he said. "I'll listen."

Mrs. Mankowitz stared out the window at the tenements of Coney Island and stroked the cat in her lap. "Have you ever felt that something was missing from your life? Some sort of magic?"

Mr. Lutz looked puzzled. "Magic? Rabbits from a hat, you mean? The world is the world. There's no magic."

"Hmm," said Mrs. Mankowitz, still staring out the window, "of that I'm not so sure."

The next morning, while at work in the fish market, Mr. Lutz had a surprise. In the back of the shop, on ice but still miraculously breathing, was the most beautiful salmon he had ever seen. Mr. Lutz stared and took a deep breath.

It was just then that the owner, Mr. Finback, came in from the freezer room. "And you, Harry," he asked, "so today is a holiday?"

"I was just admiring," Mr. Lutz said, gesturing to the salmon.

"A fish, Harry? You were admiring a fish? Forty years working here and you're admiring?"

"If you'd only look," Mr. Lutz pleaded, "you'd see. Look at those eyes, that shape, that skin!"

"I'm looking, Harry, I'm looking. And what I'm seeing, Harry, is that it's going to make one fine lox." With that Mr. Finback turned on his heels and reentered the freezer.

"Mr. Finback," Harry Lutz thought to himself, "how could you? You're a monster, a barbarian, a...a...a cannibal!"

That night Mr. Lutz couldn't sleep. He donned his robe and visited Mrs. Mankowitz. Sarah heard them talking and woke up too.

Hunched over a glass of tea and a piece of homemade strudel, Mr. Lutz told them both about the wondrous salmon.

Mrs. Mankowitz's eyes began to sparkle. "What are we going to do?" she said.

"Do?" asked Mr. Lutz dully.

"Do, Grandma?" asked Sarah.

Mrs. Mankowitz pushed back her chair. She stood. She gestured with both hands. "So, you two will sit like dishrags when there's a job to be done? Lutz, Sarah— we'll save that salmon!"

Mrs. Mankowitz, Mr. Lutz, and Sarah stole out into the dark, moonless night and made their way across the sleeping streets of Coney Island.

Mr. Lutz's slippers slapped against the sidewalk. Mrs. Mankowitz, who strode ahead, turned toward him. "Shh," she whispered, "shhhh." Sarah walked on tiptoe.

In the alley behind the fish market, Mr. Lutz found a garbage can and rolled it carefully beneath a window. Sarah climbed up and pried open the window while Mrs. Mankowitz held her granddaughter's ankles.

As soft as a whisper, they climbed in.

"Ah," said Mrs. Mankowitz.

"Ooo," said Sarah.

"You see?" said Mr. Lutz.

The salmon lay shining brightly on the ice, more beautiful than ever. But it was breathing with difficulty now and gazed sadly toward them.

"Have we come in time?" whispered Mrs. Mankowitz. "Have we come in time?"

Mrs. Mankowitz climbed out the window and helped Sarah out. Then she reached up her arms for the fish. "Gently, Mr. Lutz," she whispered, "like a baby."

Mr. Lutz handed down the salmon and then climbed backward out the window, his slippered foot reaching anxiously for the top of the can. He touched it—and then, with a crash, with a thunderthump, with a rumbling clang, the can fell over and bounced down the alley.

Mr. Lutz landed on his bottom. Sheepishly, he looked up and said, "So, a person is supposed to be perfect?"

There was no time for Mrs. Mankowitz to answer. An upstairs window was flung open. Mr. Finback's face thrust out.

Down the streets they ran.

"To the beach!" called Mrs. Mankowitz.

"Hurry!" urged Mr. Lutz, and grabbed Sarah's hand.

"Thief!" yelled Mr. Finback. "My salmon! Mine!" He clattered down the stairs and dashed after them.

In the ruckus, lights flicked on. Faces peered out.

One by one—in nightgowns, in pajamas, in underwear too—they joined Mr. Finback's chase, each one calling "Thief! Thief! Salmon thief!" until all of Coney Island was in hot, sleep-bumbling pursuit.

Beneath the black and moonless sky, across the wide, dark sand, toward the massive ocean and thundering waves, Mrs. Mankowitz and Mr. Lutz and Sarah ran on, the crowd roaring behind them.

The salmon, smelling the salt of the sea, smiled and began to wriggle and twist and flip, just like a person who is very happy. Mrs. Mankowitz did what she could to hold on.

At last, breathless and sloshing ankle-deep in the water, Mrs. Mankowitz opened her arms and the salmon slipped into the sea.

As Mrs. Mankowitz watched, as Sarah and Mr. Lutz
watched, as all of Coney Island watched, the salmon swam,
rose, and then rose again. It leaped. It pranced. It swiveled
in silvery arcs that grew higher and higher as it moved
farther out to sea.

Then, in one final fish-flipping leap, the salmon soared.
It rose and rose, until at last it hung, curled and poised—
a gleaming crescent moon.

"Wondrous," breathed Mrs. Mankowitz.

"Glorious," said Mr. Lutz.

"Hurray!" said Sarah.

All of Coney Island said, "Ahhh"—all except Mr. Finback,
who, with his mouth gaping open, stood speechless.

Mrs. Mankowitz turned toward Mr. Lutz. "Still you think
there's no magic in the world?"

Mr. Lutz shrugged his shoulders and smiled. "So, maybe
I was wrong?"

The salmon moon gazed down. It saw all of Coney Island begin to drift sleepily home. It saw Mr. Finback finally close his mouth. It saw the lights that had been flicked on go out again, one by one.

And on the beach, now alone, it saw Sarah and Mr. Lutz and Mrs. Mankowitz. They were moving in a circle, singing softly to themselves and dancing, their hands held high.

The salmon moon bathed them in its light.